PRAISE FOR SW

'**Hilarious!** Wonderfully warm illustrations . . .
full of surprises.'
Sarah McIntyre

'**A winner.**'
Guardian

'Every page is **packed with laughs**.'
Michelle Robinson

'Children will undoubtedly **love** this . . .
will have them **giggling** throughout.'
Bookbag

'**Full of laughs.**'
Tom Fletcher

'**Perfect** for fans of Pamela Butchart
and Alex T. Smith.'
Book Lover Jo

FABER has published children's books since 1929. T. S. Eliot's *Old Possum's Book of Practical Cats* and Ted Hughes' *The Iron Man* were amongst the first. Our catalogue at the time said that 'it is by reading such books that children learn the difference between the shoddy and the genuine'. We still believe in the power of reading to transform children's lives. All our books are chosen with the express intention of growing a love of reading, a thirst for knowledge and to cultivate empathy. We pride ourselves on responsible editing. Last but not least, we believe in kind and inclusive books in which all children feel represented and important.

SWAPNA HADDOW is the award-winning author of the Dave Pigeon and Bad Panda series. She lives in New Zealand with her husband, son and their dog, Archie.

SHEENA DEMPSEY is the award-winning illustrator of the Dave Pigeon and Bad Panda series. She lives in Kent with her partner, Mick, and their greyhound, Sandy.

ALSO BY SWAPNA AND SHEENA

Dave Pigeon

Dave Pigeon (Nuggets!)

Dave Pigeon (Racer!)

Dave Pigeon (Royal Coo!)

BAD Panda

Swapna Haddow SHEENA DEMPSEY

faber

First published in the UK in 2021
First published in the US in 2021
by Faber and Faber Limited
Bloomsbury House
74–77 Great Russell Street
London WC1B 3DA
faberchildrens.co.uk

Typeset in Sweater School by Faber
This font has been specially chosen to support reading

Printed and bound by Short Run Press Ltd, Exeter, UK

A CIP record for this book is available from the British Library

ISBN 978–0–571–35241–8

6 8 10 9 7

For Ockie, with love and smooshy kisses

S. H.

For Jane and Emily, with squishy panda hugs x

S. D.

Are **YOU** sick of being utterly adorable?

Tired of being cuddled and hugged?

Fed up of having your head confused for your **bottom** because you just so happen to be SOOOOPER-DOOOOOPER fluffy?

Are you making plans to build a bamboo hut, with bamboo windows, bamboo shutters and a reinforced bamboo-laser door with bamboo cannons and catapults so you can fire panda poo at the next ranger who comes along and does those schmoopy-loopy-wubbie-schnubbie-gooey-heart eyes at you because they find you **'too cute, just too darn cute'?**

1

Being Good Is Boring

Up past the gift shop and along from the monkeys, there lives a panda.

Her name is Lin, because that's what her mum called her. Actually, her mum named her

'Grrrrr-AHHHHH-RRRR-rrrrrr' but the panda keepers heard 'Lin' so that's what stuck.

That's Lin there.

Lin is an absolute rotter of a panda.

You might be wondering why a panda that cute would be a rotter? Pandas are super-duper sweethearts, right? With their super-duper kind eyes and their super-duper fluffy heads? Isn't that why everyone **loves** pandas?

Well, that's exactly why Lin was a rotter. She hated being cute. She hated it so much. In fact, Lin hated most things you would've thought a panda would love. She hated being cuddled.

She hated all the ooohhhhs and ahhhhhs and the drippy heart eyes visitors gave her as they passed by her enclosure.

She also hated a bunch of other stuff you might think a panda had no idea about.

She hated playgrounds. She hated ice cream,

even the jelly-tipped ones. She hated bubbles.

She hated snow days. She hated sand days. She

hated Sundays. She even hated cosy socks. She

hated fluffy blankets. She hated unfluffy blankets.

She hated unbluffy flankets.

She hated pizza and chips.

She hated chips and pizza.

And you reading this book right now? Well, she'd probably hate that too.

She was the sort of panda who would tell you to pull your baby sister's pigtails, steal your best friend's sweets, knock over your granddad's bike and push in front of your granny in a queue.

She was a total grotter of a rotter of a panda. And this is her story.

***

But Lin hadn't always been a rotter of a panda.

She'd been born on a fine day at a fine hour.

The panda elders had commented on this in a fine manner, at the time, especially as her big brother had been born on a stormy, icy day at the unpandaly hour of three forty-eight in the morning and had come out looking like a bag of potatoes that had been spun too fast in a washing machine.

Lin's adorable face soon became the centre of attention at the panda sanctuary where her family lived.

'Remember, you represent pandas everywhere,' her mother would tell her, and Lin knew she had to do her best to be polite and kind and smile for the visitors.

Lin washed her paws after every poo. She finished all her homework on time at Panda School and she even shared her panda cake with the pandas next door.

At first it was fun. Her face was on all the panda posters. People would bring her gifts of bamboo and carrots just for a glimpse of her lovable fluffy face or a chance to watch her do a cute roll off her hammock.

But what came easy to the other cubs was a **huge** effort for young Lin. There was absolutely nothing fun about washing your paws, handing in your homework and sharing cake with the pandas next door. (You know what is fun? Washing your homework, handing in your poo and eating all the cake.) The burden to be the best panda in the sanctuary weighed heavy on Lin like a pair of rusty anchors attached to another pair of rusty anchors attached to a pair of rusty knickers.

Lin's most favourite thing to do was to play with her big brother, Face-Like-A-Bag-Of-Potatoes. They rolled around in the dirt for hours and hours, whacking each other over the head with bamboo stems, talking about the important things like whether a panda is black and white or whether a panda is white and black and whether Dalmatian dogs were pandas who hadn't eaten enough bamboo and whether zebras were Dalmatian dogs who had eaten too much dog food.

'Let's always whack each other over the head with bamboo,' Lin said.

'Always,' Face-Like-A-Bag-Of-Potatoes replied.

But when Face-Like-A-Bag-Of-Potatoes took

a whopper panda dump in the visitor car park, the decision was made by the panda elders to keep him away from his little sister on the far side of the sanctuary, where Lin could only see him if she jumped up on the shoulders of two other pandas to peer past the bamboo trees.

(The poo was massive, just so you know. Colossal in fact. It was so gigantic that it took ninety-eight people sixty-three hours to clean it up and there is still a bit of a strange smell when you walk past the car park today.)

***

Lin watched from afar as her beloved big brother swung on tyre swings all day long and broke as much bamboo over his head as he wanted. He'd become quite the champion bamboo breaker as he spent hours and hours mastering the art. Lin felt like one thousand tiny shuai jiao wrestlers were pulling her heart apart, bit by bit.

Lin loved her brother. He was her hero. She wanted more than ever to enjoy a life like his and to be free of the pressures of being a

panda celebrity. As Face-Like-A-Bag-Of-Potatoes

flourished in his life of peace, Lin's fame grew

and grew. People visited from far and wide to

take pictures of the world's cutest panda and Lin

was no longer in control of her own life.

The people from the zoo?

Just like all the other panda cubs, Lin had been told on the very first day of Panda School that going to the zoo was like eating a chocolate sundae with pizza-flavoured sprinkles. It was the greatest gift any panda could ask for and only the best-behaved pandas got to go.

'I'm going to the zoo?' Lin exclaimed.

'You've been such a good panda,' Mama replied. 'You deserve it.'

'But what about Face-Like-A-Bag-Of-Potatoes?'

'Don't worry about your brother,' Mama said. 'He'll be just fine without you.'

Lin knew **she** wouldn't be fine without him. She pleaded with her mother and then with her father and then with the elders and then with anyone who would listen, including a flock of

chickadee birds who were sympathetic but quite busy and on their way to a family wedding.

But Lin's fate was sealed.

'Be a good panda,' the elders told Lin before packing up her bamboo suitcase and sending her on her way. 'The world wants a cute panda and this is your path.' This turned out to be the worst mistake they'd ever make after the last worst mistake they ever made which was a mistake so bad it has been removed from the panda history books.

'I don't want to leave you,' Lin howled to her beloved brother, who was clambering up the bamboo border fence to try and reach her.

'Unfortunately, you weren't blessed with a face like a bag of potatoes,' Face-Like-A-Bag-Of-Potatoes said sadly, as he fell back down on his side of the border. He peered through the long green leaves as his sister got ready to leave the sanctuary for good. 'You have to do what the elders tell you,' he called after her.

As Lin was driven away in her travel crate, she called out to Face-Like-A-Bag-Of-Potatoes, 'I'll do whatever I can to get back to you. I promise,' she cried.

2

The Nine-hour Flight
with a Talking Box

'Nǐ hǎo!'

Lin had been on the plane from the sanctuary

to the zoo for almost ten minutes, trying to

figure out how she could get back home, when

the greeting in the silence almost shocked the fur

off her bottom.

'Who's there?' she growled.

She peered through the window of her crate,

pulling up the shutter to get a clearer look.

There, across the aisle of the aeroplane, was another panda crate, with a panda inside staring straight back at her.

'I'm Fu,' the panda said, waving at Lin. He squinted his eyes to take a closer look at her.

'You're Lin! The cutest panda off of all the panda posters,' he gasped.

'You must be mistaken,' Lin said, quickly releasing the shutters on her crate. She was not in the mood to deal with fans.

'Wait,' Fu called out as the wooden panels rolled down. 'Who is "Face-Like-A-Bag-Of-Potatoes"?'

Lin caught the shutter mid fall and yanked it up.

'How do you know my brother?' she asked.

'I don't,' Fu said. 'But someone has signed the

side of your crate with mushed-up panda cake.'

Lin stretched round to look at the spot Fu was pointing to. There, scrawled in chewed-up panda cake and spit, were the words 'Face-Like-A-Bag-Of-Potatoes woz 'ere'. Lin chuckled. **Classic Face-Like-A-Bag-Of-Potatoes**, she thought.

'That's my brother,' Lin told Fu. 'He must've used his breakfast to write me a message.'

'He sounds like a top panda.'

'He is.'

Fu cleared his throat. 'You **are** Lin, aren't you?'

Lin nodded and looked down at her paws.

'Why did you say you weren't?'

Before Lin could say a word, tears rolled down her face and she bawled out how she never wanted to be a celebrity and just wanted to spend time with her brother, rolling around in the dirt.

Fu listened. He held one paw up to the wall of his crate, reaching out to Lin. 'That sucks like a mouldy bambooccino,' he said.

Fu's gentle voice calmed Lin and after she wiped away the tears soaking her fur, she reached up a paw to match Fu's.

'Tell me about your brother.' Fu smiled.

Lin regaled Fu with stories of her brother. She told him about the time Face-Like-A-Bag-Of-Potatoes did a massive poo in the car park, and when he tried to eat fifty-nine bamboo stems in one mouthful.

'I'm going to get back to my brother as soon as I can,' Lin told Fu.

'How?' Fu asked, his eyes wide.

'I don't know,' Lin admitted.

Fu thought for a moment before he said, 'I guess if being a good panda got you to the zoo, then to get home you need to be—'

Lin's snout twitched and her eyes grew bright as she could finally see a plan coming together.

'Yes?' she exclaimed, wanting to make sure that she and Fu were on the same page.

'You need to be . . .' Fu continued slowly, 'an ostrich.'

'What?'

'I mean, it could work,' Fu said.

'No, Fu!' Lin cried. She paused. 'You said being a good panda is why I'm heading to the zoo, so to go home I need to be a—'

'Fox?' Fu suggested.

'No!'

'A cushion?'

'No!'

'Oh, I got it! Is it a taco?'

'No!'

'A dog with an aptitude for maths?'

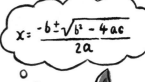

'No!'

'A tree?'

'No!'

'A bathtub full of baked beans?'

'No!'

This went for on a while.

***

'A—'

'STOP!' Lin groaned.

Fu sat back.

'I know exactly how I'm going to do it,' Lin said. 'Being a good panda is what got me sent to the zoo, so to go home I need to be a **bad** panda.' She grinned. 'I'm going to be so bad that they send me back to the sanctuary.'

Lin felt her cheeks ache, not from gritting

her teeth in anger but instead from smiling with

her new friend.

'You really are as clever as you look on the

posters,' Fu squealed.

Lin bowed her head modestly but on the inside she quite agreed with him. She regarded Fu for a moment, wondering for the first time why he was on the flight with her.

'What's your deal, Fu?' Lin asked. 'Have you been sent to the zoo for being too good too?'

Fu's grin faded. He hung his head. 'I lost my mama,' he said, in a quiet voice.

'What happened?' Lin asked, confused.

'There was an earthquake. Most of the sanctuary was crushed to bamboo pulp.' His eyes

watered. 'I survived but my mama didn't.'

Lin felt a heavy pain in her chest. She had only just met Fu, but she knew he missed his mama like she missed her brother.

And perhaps it was the way Fu was curled up, or perhaps it was the oddly familiar smell of car-park poo wafting its way across the plane from Fu's crate to hers, but there was something about Fu that reminded Lin of her brother.

'Well, it looks like we are heading to the same place,' Lin said, pointing at the matching stickers on their crates. 'So I guess we're family now.'

Fu sat up straight. His eyes brightened again and a wide,

toothy grin stretched across his fuzzy face.

'Really?' he asked, hopeful.

'Really,' Lin said, chewing up a leaf and shooting it through a hollow bamboo stick straight at Fu's crate. 'You can help me get back home if you want.'

Fu grinned adoringly at his hero and held up his paw against the wall of his crate for a panda high five.

***

Their journey ended at a city zoo. The clang and clatter of the city woke Lin and Fu, who peered curiously through the cracks in their travel crates to find out more about their noisy new home. The swish of wheels on rain-splattered tarmac reminded Lin of the waterfall at the sanctuary but it was an unfamiliar hiss that made her fur stand on end.

As Lin and Fu were wheeled in towards the main entrance of the zoo, she could see through the slats of her crate into another crate that was returning from the direction of the zoo hospital. Scaly skin rippled and shimmered green and gold through the gaps in the wooden cage, which was stamped **Danger! King Cobra** over and over and over.

The beast locked eyes with Lin. His forked tongue flicked out and licked the rim of his mouth. 'I could sssssswallow you whole if I wanted to,' said the cobra. His breath stank of dead mouse, making Lin gag.

A woman came to unlock the gate to the

zoo and peeked inside the crates. She waved at Lin and Fu, cooing with glee as she spotted the fluffy bears. She peered inside the cobra's crate and as the creature inside glared back at her, he hissed a dreadful hiss. The woman staggered back, her eyes wide with fright.

'Holy bambooccinos!' Fu whispered to Lin. 'I bet **he** knows how to be bad.'

Lin was both in awe and terrified for her life. Never before had she met someone with the level of rotterness King Cobra oozed. Lin knew right then what she was going to have to do to get back home. She was going to have to be a grotter of a rotter of a snake of a panda.

3

Pigeons Are the Worst

Lin's first night at the zoo wasn't as terrible as

she thought it was going to be. She'd been so

upset about how her fame had torn her away

from her brother that she'd forgotten there were actually some perks to being the most celebrated panda on the planet.

The panda keepers treated her to all her favourites, including panda cake and carrots. After the long flight, their hugs and snuggles were just what a homesick Lin needed, but when Fu commented on the warm glow radiating from her fluffy cheeks, Lin quickly squashed the happy feeling growing in her belly and focused back on being bad. It was the panda keepers' fault that she was miles away from Face-Like-A-Bag-Of-Potatoes and she wouldn't let anyone, **anyone**, distract her from her plan of badness.

As dawn broke, Lin looked around her new home. The zookeepers had tried hard to recreate the panda sanctuary with bamboo trees and long grass to play in. There was even a panda-sized hammock and a hill with a hidden cave beneath, which reminded Lin of the time her brother once rolled himself in grass clippings and everyone thought he was a hill.

But it wasn't home. Not even close. The entire enclosure was walled in glass for visitors to stare through and the only way in and out was via a gate at the far side of the hill which was exclusively for the zookeepers.

The gentle yawns of animals waking and the snores of the nocturnals drifting off to sleep filled the air. The sun was rising into a warm yellow sky, peppered only by the lightest of dustings of candyfloss-soft clouds.

This wasn't ideal for Lin, who would've

appreciated a more stormy, hurricaney sort of a morning to start her campaign of badness.

'Morning,' Fu called out to Lin. 'Those zookeepers are rather nice, aren't they? Look at all this yummy panda cake they've made for us.'

'Panda keepers are just pandas who gave up on their dreams of being pandas,' Lin said, determined not to be moved by the kindness but chowing down on the cake nonetheless. 'Today, Fu,' she continued, 'we must focus on being bad pandas.'

Lin paced the length of the enclosure and then climbed up on to a pile of tyres. She'd been so obedient and good for so long that being bad was not as easy as she thought it would be. As she finished up her panda cake, she automatically got up to wash her paws and had to stop herself. Bad pandas didn't wash their paws after eating. She looked down at the crumbs of cake nestled in her fur. This was what bad felt like. It was like a thousand grains of sand stuck between your fluffy toes. She wasn't used to the grittiness of

crumbs in her fur but as she wiggled her sticky paws she decided she would just have to get used to the feeling.

From her tyre throne, Lin watched Fu wash his paws in the stream that ran through their enclosure and shook her head.

'Fu,' Lin said. 'You will have to fight hard against the urge to be good. You will be no help to my escape if you don't. Perhaps a quick test will sharpen your villainous instincts.'

Lin threw up her paws. Fu was far too kind, and talking through being bad would take far too long. 'Forget the lesson,' Lin said. 'Follow my lead instead.'

A pigeon who'd landed on the gate of the panda enclosure had caught Lin's eye. Lin charged at the pigeon, her furry arms flailing and her gnashers bared. Rotterness surged through her paws, her jaws and her tummy like an explosion of watermelons in a watermelon explosion.

Fu watched

the pigeon hop down

the path. 'Maybe we aren't cut out to be

bad, Lin,' he said, thoughtfully.

'Of course we are,' Lin said, charging at

another pigeon, determined to show Fu she could

be a bad panda.

The bird didn't move. Instead, two more

feathery friends joined him.

'It's pigeons, Fu.' Lin scowled and threw up her front paws. 'They aren't really scared of anything. They eat straight out of bins and sit on fountains, even when the water smells and tastes like something that would come out of a buffalo's bottom after he's eaten gone-off cheese.'

Lin hurtled towards the pigeons again. And again. And again.

And again.

And again.

Annnnnd again.

The pigeons didn't budge.

'Mummy, look! There's a panda trying to scare those birdies!' a tiny voice squealed. 'She's sooooo cute.'

Lin and Fu turned to see a crowd of people had formed by their enclosure.

'What a naughty panda,' giggled the little girl who owned the squeally voice.

Cameras started flashing at Lin as the crowd oooohhhed and ahhhhhed over her and Fu.

'What is happening?' Lin said, looking confused.

'What?!'

The crowd grew as more onlookers snapped

photos and cooed over Lin's cuteness.

'Your badness is making them like you more,' Fu said, astounded.

'This makes no sense at all!' Lin said. 'Face-Like-A-Bag-Of-Potatoes did one bad thing and he was left alone to live a life of peace. I do a bad thing and I'm more hassled than ever?'

'Looks that way,' Fu said, waving at the crowd.

'Don't wave at them!' Lin said. 'You'll only encourage them.'

Lin crawled away from the crowd, leaving a

trail of her stinkiest farts and kicking over a pile

of bamboo.

'Sooo super-duper cute!' the crowd cooed.

'Did you see her super-duper cute kicking?'

'Gah!' Lin cried. 'The only way to get this lot

off my back is to be even badder.'

4

Being Badder Than Bad

'Here's the plan, Fu,' Lin whispered.

She and Fu were hiding in the shadows of a

grassy hillock. With no chance of getting a picture

of the cutest bad panda, the crowd had headed off around the zoo, leaving Lin and Fu to talk.

'We need to escape from our enclosure,' Lin continued. 'Out in the zoo we can be even badder than bad.' Lin smirked. She stuck her head out of the entrance to their hidden spot. There was no one there. She crawled out and signalled Fu over to follow her. 'I've been watching the zookeepers come in and out since last night,' Lin said. 'At first, I thought it would be impossible to leave our gated home but now I can see a way.'

She pointed her paw at the panda playground.

'We'll have to use the swing rope to cross the path and hide behind the bamboo pile. Then, when the keepers come in to tidy the enclosure, we sprint through the gate before sliding it shut so no one can see us.'

'I'm not sure pandas can sprint,' Fu said, making an excellent point.

Lin thought about all the times she had

sprinted in her life and then realised that that was the shortest thought she had ever had because Fu was right: she wasn't even sure she knew how to sprint.

'Fine,' Lin retorted. 'What do you suggest then?'

'We could walk straight out,' Fu said, crawling to the gate, picking the lock with his claw, swinging it open and stepping out of the enclosure.

'I suppose that could work,' Lin said, skulking after Fu.

The panda mascots walked off, shaking their heads.

Lin clenched her paws into fists and beat her chest. Then she remembered she was a panda, not a gorilla, but then remembered she didn't care and beat her chest again. 'Why won't anyone take me seriously as a bad panda?' she roared.

'I do,' Fu reassured his friend.

'Really?' Lin asked, her eyes wide and hopeful.

Fu nodded. 'I think you're the scariest panda I've ever met.'

Lin smiled at her new best friend and picked a bit of bamboo off his stumpy neck before eating it.

The two pandas continued to wander through the zoo. They walked past the big cats, banged on the windows of the tigers' enclosure, stood very still when a tiger came up to investigate

what all the banging was about and then blamed

it on a Year 1 school trip when the tiger started

asking questions.

 'Do you see what I see?'
Lin said with a wide grin as
they scrambled down the
path towards the main

entrance.

Fu followed Lin's gaze. 'Somebody dropped

their ice cream by the main gate?' he replied.

'No, Fu,' Lin said. 'I see an opportunity.'

'What are you going to do?'

'If we scare off the visitors arriving at the gate and no one ever visits again, the keepers will realise how bad I am for the zoo and send me home immediately,' Lin exclaimed. 'Hold the bao and bambooccinos, Fu. It's time to show this zoo how bad I can really be,' Lin said, her grin stretching as wide as a menacing panda grin could stretch.

'How are you going to scare the people?' Fu asked.

Lin hadn't thought that far ahead. She rustled up a plan quickly. 'We are going to stand by the main entrance and force everyone to give us their packed lunches.'

'That doesn't sound very nice at all,' Fu said. He was a panda with principles and morals and a conscience that gave him an uncomfortable feeling in the pit of his stomach when he was about to do something nasty.

'Remember, Fu, you need to fight the urge to be good and follow my lead,' Lin demanded.

'Those lunch boxes are probably filled with panda cake and bamboo sandwiches anyway and I know how much you like a panda cake bamboo sandwich.'

'OK. I'm in,' Fu said. It turned out that feeling in the pit of his stomach was actually hunger.

Come on, children. That's enough of these cute pandas. Who wants to see something scary?

We do!

Let's go and see the reptiles.

Lin was furious that the school trip hadn't been terrified at all. She was sure her growling would've had them shaking like a jelly lasagne on a trampoline but there hadn't even been the slightest quiver. She grabbed a slimy banana peel from the bin and hurled it at the next group of visitors who came through the gate.

'Oh look at this adorable panda who wants to play catch,'

a gentleman cooed
as he caught the
banana skin and
threw it back.

'What does a bad panda

have to do around here to be taken seriously?' Lin

yelled as the skin plonked directly on to Fu's head.

And that's when Lin spotted it. There, in the

reflection of the security-office windows, was a

wall of television screens. In the bottom right,

on the television, Lin could see lines and lines of

people, squealing and shrieking as they entered the reptile zone to see the King Cobra.

She remembered that dizzy feeling that had made her feel queasy on the day she was brought to the zoo and she'd been threatened by the reptile. Her fur felt icy cold again and she trembled as a shudder rolled up her back.

All of a sudden, Lin saw what she'd been doing wrong and what she had to do to make her mark as the baddest panda the world had ever seen.

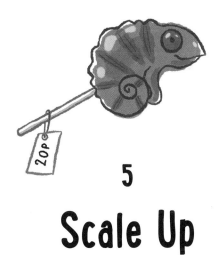

5

Scale Up

'Fu, write this down!'

'I can't write. I'm a panda.'

'Fine,' Lin said, jumping up and down. 'Just listen up.'

Fu plonked down on the pavement and gazed

up at his excited panda friend.

'It's clear that for me to be the baddest of

bad pandas, the most rotterest of the rotters,

I need to—'

'Lick a poo?'

Fu interrupted.

'No.' Lin

sighed.

'Eat an ice cream too fast and make your

brain feel like one hundred million tiny electric

eels are having a disco

in there?'

   'No.'

   'Pick your nose?'

   'No.'

       'Pick your toes?'

       'Are we seriously doing this again?'

       'I've got it!' Fu

       said,   inspired.

       'Pick someone

       else's nose?'

'NO.'

'Someone else's toes?'

'No, no, no, no, no, no, no!' Lin cried. 'I need to become a snake, obviously. It's so obvious.'

'It's not that obvious.'

'Of course it is,' Lin said.

Lin crawled over to Fu and pointed to the sky. 'What do you hear?'

The pandas sat still, their ears perked up. There, over the din of shoes slapping on the pavements and overexcited children whacking

their lunch boxes over

each other's heads,

was the faint sound of

shrieks of terror.

'Who is screaming?' Fu

exclaimed.

'Those are the people gathered in the reptile zone.' Lin grinned. 'They are visiting the snakes.'

Fu could now make out the howls of crying children, pleading to leave the reptile-filled vivarium.

'We are going to be such bad pandas, Fu,' Lin said, gleefully. 'But we need to scale up and snake up and become as bad as the cobras.'

'But the cobras are locked in the zoo too,' Fu said. He scratched his head in confusion and then his bottom (but that was because it was itchy from sitting on a woollen mitten a child had dropped on the pavement).

'Remember how I said being good got me into the zoo so being bad would get me out?' Lin said.

Fu nodded slowly.

'Well, it's the opposite for snakes obviously!'

Lin explained. 'Bad gets them in and good gets them out.'

'I suppose that makes sense,' Fu said, thoughtfully.

'Of course it does!' Lin insisted. 'Snakes are the total opposite of pandas. They are scaly and we are furry. They are small and we are big. They are carnivores and we are herbivores. They are smelly and we—'

'Only smell on Tuesdays,' Fu finished.

'Exactly.'

PANDA CHECKLIST
FOR ZOOKEEPERS

MONDAY	Cleaning	✓
TUESDAY	Panda Cake	✓
WEDNESDAY	Bathtime ✳	✓
THURSDAY	Cuddles	✓
FRIDAY	Snuggles	✓
SATURDAY	Carrots	✓
SUNDAY	More Panda Cake!	✓

I want in is what I want. I want in on your plan to escape the zoo. I'm ready to be a rotter of a panda.

You're a monkey.

Wait, Fu. Let's not be too hasty. Who says a capuchin monkey can't be a bad panda? Especially when he can get us snake costumes.

Am I in?

I admire your determination, Malo, and your ability to climb trees.

So?

Get us the snake outfits and you're in.

Of course, my leader. I'm at your service.

Why would you even want to be a panda?

I am the last of the capuchin monkeys here at the park and I am struggling to fit in with any other groups.

The rodents say I'm too big. The chimpanzees say I'm too small. The zebras say I'm too capuchin.

No more questions, Fu. You ask too many of them. You've already asked at least twenty in this story so far.

You will make a fine bad panda so long as you get us snake costumes.

I will prove myself worthy of a bad panda title, my leader.

I have the most correctomango plan to turn you into snakes.

Malo's idea was sort of brilliant. For a monkey.

Quite frankly, Lin wasn't sure why **she** hadn't

thought of the plan when she saw the little capuchin

point to the gift shop by the reptile zone on the

zoo map. The reptile gift shop had everything:

reptile-shaped frisbees,

reptile-shaped pens,

reptile-shaped hats,

reptile-shaped lollies,

reptile-shaped sausage

rolls, reptile-shaped toilet

seats, reptile-shaped reptiles, reptile-shaped bathroom tiles, reptile-shaped roof tiles and of course reptile-shaped disguises.

Lin's heart pounded in her furry chest as they hurried towards the shop in a way so as not to look like two pandas and a tiny monkey hurrying towards a gift shop.

'I'll make sure the coast is clear,' Malo whispered, scampering ahead of Lin and Fu into the store.

'Where did the tiny monkey go?' Lin asked Fu, as the two of them crept casually past a bench next to the gift shop, trying to blend in with the visitors.

Before Fu could answer, a 'psst, pssst' sound with the faint smell of monkey breath drifted towards them.

'Psssssst,' Malo whistled at the pandas.

'I'm over here!'

The whisper came from a row of soft toys hanging upside down on a silver rail by the entrance to the shop. Fu sniffed at the cuddly monkeys.

'Here!' Malo whistled again.

Lin pawed through the stuffed toys and gasped when she saw that there, hanging on the rail of cuddly monkeys, was Malo, dangling by his tail. The pandas crawled towards him, their jaws hanging open in awe at the hidden monkey. He truly was a master of camouflage.

'Come quickly, before you are spotted,' Malo said, swinging off the rail.

'That's a brilliant disguise, Malo!' Lin said to the capuchin.

'Correctomango!'

'Holy bambooccinos!' Fu exclaimed, amazed at Malo's skills. 'You really look like these toy monkeys.'

'One time a small child on a family day out accidentally bought me,' Malo confessed. 'I would have stayed with her but she insisted I ate green leaves whilst she ate all the noodles. I had to take three buses and borrow a scooter to get back to the zoo from her house.'

'This is getting out of hand. **Nobody** is respecting my badness,' Lin cried, stomping her way into the shop. 'The quicker I get into costume, the quicker I can upset the keepers and get out of here.'

Malo banged out a Christmas tune on a tambourine to distract the man with the camera as Fu and Lin made their way to the back of the gift shop where rows

of masks were stacked high on shelves.

Sitting between the lions and the blobfish was

a pile of scaly snake masks. Lin's eyes grew wide

as she swiped two from the stack and threw one

to Fu. Malo's plan to use snake costumes from

the zoo gift shop was a genius rotter idea.

The mask slipped on easily over one of Lin's

ears. But then . . . it was as ridiculous as you'd

think it would be. For a furry panda, trying to squeeze her giant fuzzy head into a teeny plastic snake mask was about as simple as jamming a pineapple into a water balloon.

'This snake mask is a bit tight, isn't it?' Lin said, rolling around on the floor as she battled with the plastic.

Malo leaped on to Lin's head and yanked hard on the bottom of the mask until it popped down over the panda's snout.

'I can't see!' Lin shouted.

'Don't worry!' Malo shouted back. 'You are looking so much more snakelike already!'

Lin grinned. At least, she tried to grin. Her face was stuffed into a mask that was too small and it was hard to know if she was grinning or grimacing.

Since they were now unable to see, Malo suggested the pandas follow their noses out of the gift shop. Only they couldn't smell much, what with their noses being squashed between their eyes under the reptile masks. It was hopeless. The pandas bashed into mugs and posters,

leaving a trail of crushed porcelain and ripped paper behind them.

Fu's big, fuzzy bottom snared a rail of children's T-shirts, flipping the metal stand they hung from upside down. Malo grabbed him as best a tiny monkey could grab a huge bear but hangers flew about the shop, clattering into a long row of snow globes, which smashed to the ground.

'Hey!' the shopkeeper yelled as he slipped in the pool of sticky snow-globe glitter. 'I've got sparkles on my bottom!'

The word 'sparkles' triggered a stampede of schoolchildren who ran towards the slippy mess, because schoolchildren can never resist running towards the action when someone yells the word 'sparkles'. (They also can't resist the words

'a jam sandwich of unicorns' so don't ever yell this during quiet reading time.)

Malo grabbed Fu and Lin and heaved them away from the children and out of the shop. Furious yells from livid shoppers, soaked in glittery snow-globe water, thundered after them.

But before the angry staff could give chase, Lin and Fu darted towards the nearest enclosure to hide. Malo swung ahead over the gate and unlocked it to let them in.

A familiar stench hit Lin straight away: dead mouse. It made her dizzy as she clawed at her mask, trying to peel a larger hole to breathe through. It was a smell that took her back to that first day she was wheeled into this zoo. The day she looked through the slats of another crate and saw the ripple of golden-green snakeskin.

6

Lin and King Cobra

King Cobra's cold eyes locked into a death-glare

staring match with Lin. Lin was ashamed to say

that she blinked first but she didn't feel too bad

to accept defeat because snakes are notorious

for not blinking much and neither one of them had said 'one-two-three-go' which we all know means it doesn't count.

The large snake rose into an upright position until the hood of his head touched the top of his glass cage, casting a long shadow over a quivering mouse that stood in front of him.

Fu stumbled over Lin's paw as he ripped at his mask, which clattered on the cold stone floor.

The sign

for the reptile

zone blinked on and

off in the shadowy cave. Fu crawled

behind Lin and Malo as the tiny monkey

arched his body forward and bared

his sharp teeth at the king.

'Lin, I'm scared,' Fu whispered,

quivering behind his friend.

'Don't worry,' Lin reassured him.

'I lost my family already. I can't lose you too,' Fu said, nuzzling into Lin's soft fur.

Lin reached round and hugged Fu. 'I'll be just fine.'

She took a deep breath and crawled forward towards the glass cage before standing tall on her back legs.

His fangs flicked out, and with one gulp he swallowed down the mouse. It was still alive and squirming inside the snake's throat as King Cobra licked his fangs.

'Why are you pandassss here?' the snake hissed. 'You're a little far from home.'

Lin's insides felt like wet spaghetti but she forced herself to stand even taller. 'I'm here to join the snakes and be the baddest bad panda this zoo has ever seen.'

A cackle of slithery sniggers echoed around

the cave as King Cobra's cronies slid towards Lin.

'You?' the cobra snarled. '**You** want to be as bad as **me**?'

'Yes,' Lin insisted.

'But you're jusssssst an overgrown teddy bear!'

'What did you say?' Lin felt her jaw tighten.

'Cobras are not cutesssssy-wutessssssy animalssssss,' King Cobra continued.

'Pandas can be just as bad as cobras,' Lin growled, through gritted teeth. 'Pandas can be right rotters if they want to be.'

'No one would ever take a panda sssssseriously,' the snake jeered. 'How could

they when pandasssss are jusssst fluffy, whuffy

ssssssnugglebeansssss to oooooh and ahhhhh

over?' He eyed the tattered masks lying on the

floor. 'You think you could sssssstick on a couple

of sssssnake masks and be as bad as—'

'As bad as who, dear?' a voice called out

from behind King Cobra.

'Mummy!' King Cobra hissed as a larger

snake slid out to join him at the glass wall.

'Cobby, I hope you aren't picking on these

lovely bears,' the snake said back.

'Cobby?' Lin repeated.

'My son has terrible manners,' the snake said as King Cobra cowered behind her. 'I'm his mum, Naja.'

If a snake could blush, King Cobra would've. But they can't so he didn't.

'Mummy, you're embarrassing me,'

King Cobra hissed through gritted fangs.

'Your mum calls you **Cobby**?' Lin said.

'Yeah, so what?' King Cobra snarled, defensively.

'Now, now, Cobbyshmoo,' Naja said, nuzzling her hood against her son's. 'Let's use our gentle, indoor vivarium voice.' She turned to Lin. 'I'm sorry about him,' she said. 'He's a bit cranky after his operation at the hospital. He's usually very nice really.'

The cranky King Cobra snarled at the

pandas but he curled up by his mum and pulled his bandaged tail round so everyone could see.

'Say sorry to the nice pandas for being so rotten,' Naja warned King Cobra.

'Soz,' the snake mumbled.

Lin looked to Fu and Malo, both of whom were staring back, astounded.

'I can't learn to be bad from you,' Lin stammered. 'You're not bad at all!'

'You thought my gentle Cobby was **bad**?' Naja asked.

'He **was** threatening to eat us,' Fu piped up.

Naja laughed, throwing her head back.

'My Cobby wouldn't hurt a fly.'

'He ate a mouse.'

Naja shrugged as though mice didn't count. 'Why would you want to learn to be bad?'

Lin slumped down to the floor. She told Naja of her plan to get back to her brother and how no one in the zoo took her badness seriously.

'If you want to learn to be bad, you've come to the wrong place,'

Naja said. 'I've been here for fifteen years and there isn't a bad animal at this zoo.'

'Apart from the humans,' King Cobra said.

'Yes, apart from the humans,' Naja agreed. 'A granny came in the other day and poked poor Cobby's tail with an umbrella,' she said, explaining King Cobra's injury.

'Ouch,' Fu said, sympathetically.

'I hate it when the people visit,' Naja said. 'They constantly tap on the glass, disrupting my naps. And how is one supposed to get to the end of a good spy novel with all that tapping?'

'The flash on the cameras hurts my eyes

when they take photos,'

King Cobra admitted. 'And sometimes I haven't had a chance to change my skin. I can't bear to think of all the terrible pictures of me out there.'

'That doesn't seem fair,' Lin said. She felt a rage in her tummy erupting, swelling inside her like an angry hippo trapped in a vending machine. This wasn't right. The zoo should be for the animals. Lin couldn't believe she had been ripped away from her brother just to sit in a glass cage for humans to gawp at her all day long.

'I heard the lemurs complaining that they were being kept up all day because of the noise of visitors,' Malo chimed in.

'And sometimes the children draw thank you cards but they never address them to us,' a snake piped up from a neighbouring tank.

'If you want to be bad,' Naja declared, 'you should find a way to turn this zoo on its head

and **really** annoy the zookeepers.'

A family of tourists interrupted the animals as they arrived at the reptile enclosure to take pictures. The snakes were right. They tapped on the glass walls and the flash stung Lin's eyes.

Lin's paws closed tight.

'Look at this cute cuddly bear, Daddy,' a little girl said as they strolled out. 'She's a big, harmless fluffy-wuffy bear.'

Lin's fists clenched tighter.

Nobody called Lin a fluffy-wuffy bear.

NOBODY.

7

Rampage!

WE ARE TAKING BACK THE ZOO!

Lin roared so ferociously that for a moment, the

panda elders who lived halfway across the world

stopped their bamboo munching and looked up at

the skies, wondering if that was their Lin making

that awful racket.

Lin threw herself at the snakes' vivarium, shaking the entire wall of glass. She then flicked out a claw into the silver lock and opened the glass door.

'What **isssss** ssssshe doing?!' King Cobra hissed, rubbing his head with his bandaged tail.

'She's releasing the animals!' Naja cried as they watched Lin cross the path to the aviary and claw off the netting that bound the birds in.

'She's doing a bad thing. A really, really bad thing,' Malo said, impressed. 'The humans are

going to be so annoyed.'

Animals charged out of their enclosures, confused, clawing and growling, slithering and twittering.

'GET TO SAFETY!' the zoo staff shrieked.

Visitors raced to climb into the animals' now-empty pens. Wide-eyed and terrified, they locked themselves in, away from the animals.

As Lin made her way across the zoo, releasing the inhabitants from their enclosures, she shouted to her fellow animals, 'Who here is sick of being ogled at all day long?'

The animals roared, hissed, crowed, barked, heehawed and purred back a resounding 'WE ARE!'

'And who here is fed up of being stuck in their enclosure and just wants to wander around and lie on the pavement from time to time?' Lin continued.

Again, the animals roared, hissed, crowed, barked, heehawed and purred back.

'And who here thinks we should all have ice creams?' Malo screeched.

There weren't so many cheers for this one because ice cream upset some of the animals' tummies and some of them preferred candyfloss anyway.

'And who here,' Lin went on, 'thinks that being free in the zoo is the way it should be so long as we agree not to eat each other?'

There was a moment of silence as they considered not eating each other and a tiger released a penguin from its jaws before there was an eruption of roars, hisses, crows, barks, heehaws and purrs of agreement.

Fu scrambled over to his best friend and hugged her hard. 'You are a hero,' he said. Lin shut her eyes as he squeezed her hard and she felt like she was back with her brother.

A slow smile stretched across Lin's face. The zoo looked like it had been whizzed around in a giant zoo blender. Animals were out. People were in. It felt right. And what's more, Lin knew this wouldn't go down well with the zookeepers. If this didn't make the people realise Lin was a rotter of a panda, she wasn't sure what would. She knew she would be back with her brother in no time.

A lion climbed up on to a large abandoned pushchair as the animals gathered round, much like they would have done in the Serengeti, or if someone was handing out unlimited free lollies and everyone was ignoring the rules of queuing.

Seriously?

Yes. A bunch of children from a local primary school named me.

I'm sorry.

I got off easy. I hear one child tried to name a pigeon Prince Googleybrain Sizzlepants Ninja Mallet-Face Wheely Shmeely Pancakeness Snotball Jelly, once.

Lin smiled at the kind lion before turning to watch the zoo staff. She tapped her claws impatiently on the pavement as she waited for them to announce her as the most terrible panda of all time before shipping her off straight back to the sanctuary.

Tap, tap

You mean the animals wandering free and the humans watching from the enclosures?

Yes. That's how a zoo should be.

What a cute idea!

Well done to Lin, the cleverest and cutest panda on the planet.

What is going on?! I wrecked the entire zoo and everyone's happy with me?

Even when you're bad, Lin, somehow you are still very good.

8

The Baddest of the Bad

So, my fellow rotters, Lin is now the most celebrated animal at the zoo. She tried to shed her celebrity but became more famous in the process. It's not all bad because she has lots of new friends and, of course, her best friend Fu. And she can flop down on the pavement whenever she feels like it.

But she's still more determined than ever to be **even** badder so she can get back to her brother.

She's going to prove to everyone that she's the baddest baddie of a rotter of a panda of them all. You'll see. She's already making her plans. She'll be the worst of the worst. The most feared bear the world has ever known. A supreme ferocious force—

Come on, kids, everyone stand still as the pandas wander around and I'll get a picture.

Grrrrrrrrr.

How cute. Can all the children growl too please?